Little Rebel

Little Rebel is first published in English in the United Kingdom in 2021 by Corylus Books Ltd, and was originally published in French as *La Petite Gauloise* in 2018 by La Manufacture de livres.

Cover art by Barry McKay

Corylus Books Ltd

corylusbooks.com

'The present instruction is intended to bring together in one single document the measures designed to combat the terrorist threat, and to explain how they relate to the National Security Alert System, and the Education Ministry's Crisis Management Procedures. It replaces the three directives cited heretofore, which are hereby annulled. Only the directive n° 2015-205 of 25 November 2015 relative to the Emergency Situation Safety Procedure (ESSP) remains in force.'

Official Bulletin of the French Education Ministry, 13 April 2017.

'This perfectly formed democracy constructs its own inconceivable enemy, namely terrorism. It wishes, in other words, to be judged on its enemies rather than on its achievements.'

Guy Debord, Notes on the Society of the Spectacle (1988)

'Maybe I've got it wrong. But I continue to believe that we are all in danger.'

Pier Paolo Pasolini, last interview, given on the eve of his death, 1 November 1975.

1

The reason why the head of Mokrane Méguelati, a police inspector attached to the regional office of the French Directorate for Internal Security, has just exploded under the impact of a 12mm calibre bullet, fired at an initial speed of 380 metres per second from the Taurus 51cm barrel pump-action shotgun of local police officer Sergeant Richard Garcia, is very probably linked to distant geopolitical conflicts. Conflicts playing themselves out thousands of miles away from this suburb perched high on a hill overlooking this port city in the west of France, a city now gripped in a heat wave, and which is known for its appallingly high levels of unemployment, the slow death of its shipyards and its reconstruction in an elegant Stalinist style after the Allied bombings of 1944.

Still, there's now a lot of brain tissue spread over the tarmac of this hilly street, renamed rue Jean-Pierre Stirbois in honour of the National Front's former Secretary General by the city's newly elected mayor – a member of the Patriotic Bloc party – but which many local residents, in their indifference to the new regime up at City Hall, continue to refer to as rue Emile-Pouget, named after a long gone anarcho-communist.

'You saw that, didn't you, Cindy?! You saw there was nothing else I could do?! I mean a fucking Arab running towards us, waving his arms about, with a gun in his hand. And just after we got that call about the shooting in the area! You saw, didn't you, the way that fucking Arab was waving his arms about? We had every right to shoot, didn't we?' asks Sergeant Richard Garcia anxiously.

Cindy Lefèvre sighs with relief, despite the presence of Mokrane Méguelati's corpse, and the reek of Richard Garcia's body odour. The thing is, Cindy Lefèvre had been rather scared when she saw an Arab appearing out of nowhere just a few yards in front of them, waving his arms about, with a gun in his hand, even though he was actually quite cute judging by his reflection in the headlights of their Dacia Duster 4x4, marked *Municipal Police*. She had been the one driving on account of the fact that Sergeant Richard Garcia, who would normally never let a bird drive, is going through a bit of a conjugal crisis right now, and spends his time speaking to his wife or texting her on his mobile.

Cindy Lefèvre also sighs from fatigue.

It's been five years since Cindy Lefèvre joined the local police force in order to earn a living while studying law in the hope of passing her Category A National Police Force Exam. But as time goes by, Cindy Lefèvre finds herself increasingly exhausted and she's already failed that exam – twice. To add insult to injury, since the Patriotic Bloc got in at City Hall they've started recruiting guys like Richard Garcia as policemen, ex-servicemen the army no longer wants but who are cousins or brothers-in-law of somebody in the mayor's office. Pains in the neck, cretins, not nasty – well not *necessarily* nasty – but idiots all the same. Like this Richard Garcia who rushed over here when HQ told them about the shooting – 'the lads in the Serious Crimes Unit will need back-up' – whereas 'the lads in the Serious Crimes Unit' think Sergeant Richard Garcia is nothing but an idiot, a pest and an interfering arse-licker.

Lights are already being switched on all down the rue Jean-Pierre Stirbois (formerly the rue Emile-Pouget). 'The 800', as this part of town is called, is inhabited by nice, easily frightened pensioners and lower middle-class people, who live in detached houses that have seen better days, just a few hundred metres from a row of tower blocks with a bad reputation. It's a kind of Indian reservation full of local young drug addicts, radicalised psychopaths, benefit junkies, women in turbans, and blokes who look like they'd slit a priest's throat given half the chance, or else mow down fans at a rock concert with a machine gun, or drive a 19-tonne truck through a crowd of people on a seafront on the evening of Bastille Day.

It's 40 minutes past midnight, Cindy Lefèvre tells herself.

Meanwhile, Sergeant Garcia tries to remember the procedure to be followed in this kind of situation. What with his marital problems, the two cartridges ejected from his Taurus ST12 tactical pump-action shotgun which testify to the fact that he did indeed fire but missed the target with his first shot, and the corpse of the fucking Arab who's lost his face, towards which Cindy Lefèvre advances cautiously, her 7.65 calibre PA Unique police pistol clutched in her hand, Sergeant Richard Garcia is a little lost. Despite appearances, and contrary to what he would have his mates in the Serious Crimes Unit think, he never once found himself in the front line with the Special Forces during his entire military career.

Sergeant Richard Garcia, who sees himself these days as a defender of the West against the Great Replacement (he's been reading the claims of Renaud Camus on the internet), ought to be pleased that he's killed an armed Arab who was very probably a left-wing Islamist terrorist.

In reality, however, Sergeant Richard Garcia feels upset more than anything, even slightly nauseous, at the sight of the corpse's face that he's blown wide open, illuminated by the Duster's headlights. Sergeant Richard Garcia tries to put his anguish into words, following the recommendations of his psychiatrist, a woman he goes to see every week on his wife's suggestion.

'I'm a little upset, and even slightly nauseous,' he announces into the heat of the night, which smells of the salt and the oil rising from the terminals of this port city at the bottom of the hill.

'What's that you're prattling on about?' asks Cindy Lefèvre, who is now leaning over the Arab's faceless corpse.

Sergeant Richard Garcia is not at all sure whether she has the right to go interfering with the body of that dead would-be terrorist before the experts get here. But Cindy Lefèvre must know what she's doing.

After all, Cindy Lefèvre sits exams.

'What's going on? Was that shooting I heard just now?' a pensioner asks them suddenly, with a voice that sounds like he's under siege, looking down at them from the skylight window of his solid, stone-clad detached house.

'Stay indoors, sir, it's safer!' orders Sergeant Richard Garcia, in a voice that he wishes sounded more virile, but which veers pathetically off towards high-pitched, on account of his anxiety.

'Is it those tower blocks again? ISIS? CGT union troublemakers?' The doddery old resident of 424 rue Jean-Pierre Stirbois (formerly rue Emile-Pouget) continues in his best siege-mentality voice.

Sergeant Richard Garcia doesn't answer him. Sergeant Richard Garcia looks at Cindy Lefèvre, who is now kneeling over the corpse. Sergeant Richard Garcia admires Cindy Lefèvre's rather large rump, its curves sumptuously embraced by the navy blue combat trousers of her uniform. A rather large rump it is too, but just the kind he likes. He feels the first vague stirrings of a hard-on; it's been months since his wife has let him have sex with her, and Cindy Lefèvre doesn't just have a voluptuous arse – you can have a conversation with her, as well.

Sergeant Richard Garcia suddenly imagines himself approaching her there, in the night, and sticking it up her while standing over the sodding dead Arab, the pair of them going at it under the lustful eye of that pensioner who thinks he's under siege, the entire scene caught in the Duster's headlights, high above the brightly lit port city which smells of salt and oil. Sometimes his fantasies are like something out of a Pasolini film.

Sergeant Richard Garcia has a proper hard-on now, but

his erection suddenly vanishes into the night, along with the dreamlike vision of Cindy Lefèvre's ample behind, when Cindy Lefèvre gets to her feet and turning towards him, says,

'Richard, I think you just shot a cop.'

2

It is at this point that we must say goodbye to Sergeant Richard Garcia and his colleague Cindy Lefèvre. Theirs is only a minor role in our story; we have included them merely in order to help the reader better understand the historical period, the place, and the violent atmosphere of both.

If the reader were really keen to know more, an omniscient narrator could reveal that in the years following the above related incident, Cindy Lefèvre, tired of failing her police officer's exams, will leave the port city after marrying a general practitioner ten years her junior, and will go to live with him in a village somewhere in the South of France. In the 2020s Cindy Lefèvre will publish two volumes of poetry with a leading Parisian publisher, which will be well received by connoisseurs of the genre.

Sergeant Richard Garcia will not be prosecuted for blowing Captain Mokrane Méguelati's head off. Nevertheless, the Patriotic Bloc bigwigs up at City Hall, worried about their public image, will force him to resign from the municipal police force just a few months later. Sergeant Richard Garcia will become a security guard at the Blue Note, one of the port's nightclubs, located in the trendy part of the city near the old arsenal. During a student party held at the club, the security guard Richard Garcia will meet a girl enrolled on a Master's programme in international law whom he will save from being gang raped by a group of business school students who've drunk too much wine, and whose ideas of sex have been formed at a very early age, thanks to websites such as YouPorn and iWank. Richard Garcia will kick fifty shades of shit out of them and will help the crying girl, who will have a split lip, and will be crawling around on the floor between two large wheelie bins when he comes to her rescue, to put her clothes back on.

Despite their difference in social class, the girl will fall in love with the divorced security guard, and change him forever. Richard Garcia will shed both four stone and his extreme right wing views. He will follow his newfound love, now an expert in NGO law, as she travels the world on various humanitarian missions. The last we heard, Richard Garcia was helping out at Idomeni, a transit camp for migrants in Macedonia.

On the other hand, it may well interest the reader to know just what Inspector Mokrane Méguelati of the French Directorate for Internal Security was doing out at The 800, on a June evening as soft and gentle as the first stirrings of love in a song by Charles Trenet, before having his face ripped off by a .12 calibre bullet and receiving full posthumous honours from the local *Préfet* and the French Interior Minister during a moving ceremony at which a letter will be read out, signed by the President himself, who will be unable to attend, owing to an official visit he will be undertaking at the same time in some oil-rich emirate.

3

The reason why Inspector Mokrane Méguelati of the French Directorate for Internal Security was on his way to a meeting with an informant that very evening can no doubt be found not just in distant geopolitical conflicts, but also, and more especially, in the specific form those conflicts have taken both in the West in general and in this large port city in western France in particular.

Everyone has a view on the whys and wherefores. Inspector Mokrane Méguelati also has his own particular opinion on the issue, even though he's rarely asked for it – his opinion that is – which is really quite astonishing when you consider that Inspector Mokrane Méguelati is an Arab and a Muslim (not a practising Muslim, granted, but a Muslim nevertheless), and that he's on the front line of what is commonly known as the *war against terrorism*.

No, nobody ever asks him for his opinion, he thinks to himself as he parks his car near the city's Saint-François Hill. Tonight he's at the wheel of his own family car, a Volvo S40 with little girls' toys strewn across the back seat and a Hand of Fatima hanging from the rear-view mirror. Nobody ever asks him for his opinion to his face, but after every terrorist attack they ask him to explain himself – although never in so many words.

Not his colleagues of the French Directorate for Internal

Security of course, but plenty of those dickhead journalists or politicians who shape public opinion and who raise their hysterical voices to ask why the Muslims of France aren't holding mass protests to distance themselves from the atrocities perpetrated in the name of Islam.

You bunch of ignorant pricks – thinks Mokrane Méguelati as he checks how many rounds he has left in the chamber of his .45 calibre ACP Glock 41 – when they're not actually dying themselves as a result of such atrocities, they don't necessarily have the time to demonstrate: they may be injured, or they may be a member of a medical team caring for the injured, or one of the teachers trying to explain what happened to a classroom full of kids the next morning, or one of the cleaning ladies mopping up the blood the day after, or one of the women making up your stupid face before you go sounding off on one of those 24-hour TV news channels. They may even be one of the cops who go hunting the terrorists and get themselves killed for their trouble.

Which happens to be why this very evening Mokrane Méguelati has an appointment with his informant Abdul Slimane in a dodgy café which they don't usually visit, located in the midst of the labyrinthine network of side streets and seventeenth-century fortifications on the south side of The 800. Near the Saint-François Hill, if you know where that is.

Inspector Mokrane Méguelati didn't much care for the tone of Abdul Slimane's voice when he called him in a bit of a panic at around 11.30 in the evening. Inspector Mokrane Méguelati had just arrived home in the suburb of Sainte-Marguerite, a reasonably chic area of this port city, overlooking the sea. Inspector Mokrane Méguelati has forty years left on the mortgage he took out to buy his house – and that's after his wife Fadila managed to obtain an attractive interest rate at the bank where she works. But it's worth the expense, just to be able to raise his two daughters here, in this quiet area notable for its unobstructed view of the ocean and its healthy sea air, living next door to people who are well-off, liberal-minded

Catholics, who generally vote Centre-Right and who pretend not to notice that Inspector Mokrane Méguelati, his wife Fadila and their two daughters Warda and Juliette, are... a bit... well, Arabic really. Most importantly, there's the sound the tide makes as it washes over the pebbled beach, a sound which has quite a calming influence on the Méguelati household and which sends certain members of that very household into contemplative reveries worthy of nineteenth-century Romantic poets, especially on long hot summer evenings.

'Bar de l'Amitié, midnight, Mokrane. And don't be late!' Abdul said.

'Why can't we meet in the centre of town, like we usually do?'

'Because they smell a rat, Mokrane, I'm sure of it! I'd rather stay close to home. I'm onto something big. If I go wandering around the town centre tonight, our bearded brethren'll get wind of it and I'll end up getting my throat cut. You know I've only got ten minutes to show my face whenever they call me.'

'What are you onto?'

'I can't tell you over the phone, Mokrane. My phone might have been tapped, your phone might have been tapped, all our phones might have been tapped, and not by the people you think. For all you know, your phone might have been tapped by your colleagues, your colleagues might have had their phones tapped by our bearded brethren and I...'

'Abdul?'

'Yeah?'

'Abdul, will you just calm down a minute?'

With Abdul Slimane, you never quite know how seriously to take his paranoia, given that he spends most of his time snorting cocaine (although he does occasionally find the time to eat some of his mother's home-made hummus). On top of which, Abdul Slimane may very well be right to be scared shitless. After ten years of working for various intelligence services, Inspector Mokrane Méguelati knows only too well that counter-terrorism often works in remarkably mysterious ways.

Inspector Mokrane Méguelati is not very proud of the manner in which he turned Abdul into an informant two years ago, but all's fair in love and war as they say, and this is apparently what we're in; a war.

Abdul had been on the radar of the anti-terrorism boys since January 2015. A brother in Syria, two burka-clad sisters and the man himself, as pally as you like with the Salafist Imam, a man of hard-line views on Sharia Law, of the mosque in the Rue Aristote, over at The 800. Problem was, the cops who'd hacked into his computer had found he spent most of his time watching hard-core gay porn rather than jihadist sites (needless to say, the jihadist sites were also hard-core, although not quite in the same way).

Inspector Mokrane Méguelati had mentioned this to his chief, but all he'd got in return was a 'Mmm yeah. Maybe. Who knows? Nobody gives a shit if he's queer, right? And anyway, your Slimane bloke's only got a very small, walk-on part in this war – more fourth fiddle than second. Do you fancy going after his ass? After all, you're all a bit gay aren't you, you Arabs? Eh, calm down, Mokrane, for fuck's sake! I'm only having a laugh! Look, I don't buy it. But it's your call, OK?'

Inspector Mokrane Méguelati had let his instinct guide him as he'd tracked Abdul. He discovered that now and again Abdul would pass a message on from the Imam at the Rue Aristote to other suspicious Imams in the Paris area. Once Abdul met the Imam in question and told him what he'd been instructed to say, without the police surveillance team managing to get even a half-decent recording of their conversation with their high-tech microphones, Abdul Slimane would head off towards the gare Saint-Lazare. The guys from the police surveillance team, looking less than pleased with themselves, would suggest going for a bite to eat together. Surely Inspector Mokrane Méguelati could catch a later train home? And the *plat du jour* at Germaine's little place, over at la Dalle d'Argenteuil, was to die for.

'It's pork and lentils today, isn't it, Lolo?'

'I think so, yeah.'

Sometimes Inspector Mokrane Méguelati accepted his colleagues' invitation and ate the pork that he was forbidden to touch by a religion that he didn't really give a toss about. In fact, he tended to find it even more succulent when it was *haram* – strictly prohibited under Islamic law – and washed down with a bottle of Côtes du Rhône that had been treated with sulphites, but was pretty strong stuff nevertheless. On other occasions, however, he preferred to head off to tail Abdul who was bound to crack sooner or later, what with his ill-assumed sexuality.

This is indeed what eventually happened one evening before the last train left for the big port city in the West, near the gare Saint-Lazare, among the sex shops and brothels of the rue de Budapest to be precise, when Abdul emerged from a sauna opposite which Inspector Mokrane Méguelati had positioned himself, sitting at a table behind a bottle of Vittel. The first set of photos he'd captured with his smartphone had been nothing to write home about. But then Abdul, no doubt all hot and bothered, had committed a rather unfortunate indiscretion, going down on a middle manager who had left the sauna with him, right there, in the filthy, stinking entrance to some courtyard.

Another set of photos, much more compromising this time. Taken by surprise, Abdul got to his feet brandishing a knife, but calmed down once he saw the Glock 41 and the police ID card. The middle manager hadn't even managed to come in the mouth of this young man who was in the process of being radicalised, but he was only too happy to zip his flies back up, and run off towards the station on a nod from the inspector, whose silence had worried him somewhat, and catch his train back to his home in the suburbs where he'd eventually be able to forget about the entire incident by watching some disturbing news report on TV.

The deal had been put to Abdul Slimane in the second-class carriage of a train heading back to the port city.

'Either you work for me from now on, my little Slimane,

or else everybody on social media gets to see how good you are at giving head. And don't say I can't do that, because I can do whatever I like, since I work in counter-terrorism and in counter-terrorism we can do whatever we like. You shouldn't have attacked democracy, Slimane, because when you do that, she stops being so democratic. A shame, but that's the way it is. I know you're not a big shot or anything, but as the little errand boy you might get to hear things, especially since, although you're basically just a smack-head faggot, you do spend most of your time at the Rue Aristote mosque, but of course that's your business.'

Inspector Mokrane Méguelati was fifteen years old on 11th September 2001. His father owned a corner shop in a dormitory town in the greater Paris area where he sold pasta or milk to people who didn't have the time to go to the supermarket after three hours' commuting on the clapped-out public transport network. He had said to Mokrane, 'My son, you'd better work hard at school because things aren't going to be easy for people like us in the years to come.'

Mokrane Méguelati had watched over and over again the Twin Towers come crashing down on the little TV in his father's grocery store, not daring to admit that he had been struck by the sheer aesthetic beauty of the event, a beauty he found vastly superior to that of any disaster movie. But he understood what his father was trying to tell him and decided to join the police, moved by the rather romantic notion that this might help protect members of his community from the kind of sweeping generalisations which would no doubt be used to attack them in the forthcoming weeks and months.

And so, nearly twenty years later, one interminable, balmy June evening, this vocation of his sees Inspector Mokrane Méguelati enter the poorly lit Bar de l'Amitié with its old-fashioned and rather touching décor (they've even got table football). *How long has it been*, Inspector Mokrane Méguelati wonders, *since I last played table football*? It's so scary, how quickly time passes; table football belongs to the France of old, to his childhood, a time when everything was so wonderfully simple, a time spent chewing gum and staring at that pencil stuck behind his dad's ear. *How the hell did we get where we are today? But I'm not here to ask questions like that.*

There are only two other people in the bar – the owner, an obese Tunisian, and Abdul Slimane, nothing but skin and bone, sitting there, pupils dilated, behind an alcohol-free beer at a table right at the back. Could be a trap, Inspector Mokrane Méguelati's canny cop's sixth sense whispers into his ear.

Which is exactly what it is.

That prick Abdul has been followed. Two bearded blokes in djellabas enter the bar. It's not so much the djellabas that make Inspector Mokrane Méguelati nervous. After all, he sometimes wears one himself, along with Fadila and the girls, on a Sunday, to watch the sea from their living room in Sainte-Marguerite. It's very comfortable. No, what makes Inspector Mokrane Méguelati nervous are the two Kalashnikovs the bearded blokes are pointing at them.

'Shit!' he exclaims, although he's not usually given to swearing.

'No!' screams Abdul Slimane, shitting himself.

'*Weld el kahba!*' yells the obese Tunisian who runs the bar.

Inspector Mokrane Méguelati doesn't hesitate. He reaches for his Glock 41 as he tips over a table behind which he takes cover, but which is immediately blown to pieces by a hail of bullets from the Kalashnikovs.

Inspector Mokrane Méguelati returns fire, shooting blindly, emptying half his magazine while further bursts from the Kalashnikovs transform the Bar de l'Amitié into a scene from Mossoul, Alep or Kobani – you know what I mean, one of those places where the Christian West is bravely resisting Islamic barbarity, as someone from, say, the Patriotic Bloc might put it, before denying access to the city's crèches for the children of unemployed parents.

The shooting stops.

Inspector Mokrane Méguelati raises his head slowly from

behind the red Formica table, which is now full of 7.62mm-sized holes and would therefore make a great piece for a contemporary art exhibition in the city's Arts Centre which has just had its funding cancelled.

The two bearded blokes are quite badly wounded and are crawling around amid shards of glass from the bar's shattered front window. Inspector Mokrane Méguelati stands up. He shoots both men dead because, well, because it's a bit much really, going round behaving like that – one with a bullet in the back of the head, and the other with a bullet right between his eyes.

Otherwise, the Tunisian's dead, lying there amid broken bottles that once contained the kind of old-fashioned liqueurs that these days you can only get in bars that are well off the beaten track. As for Abdul Slimane, he's sitting on the floor, smelling of blood and shit. He simply says, with a vacant look in his eyes,

'They're planning something for tomorrow.'

'Where?'

'In town, I think.'

'Where in town?'

'I've no idea. They said it would be a big surprise. Get an ambulance, I'm dying.'

The thing that most disturbs Inspector Mokrane Méguelati is the smell of Abdul Slimane's shit. It's so bad he can't concentrate. He tries to think of the salt-tinged sea spray at Sainte-Marguerite, and his girls' toys lying on the back seat of his Volvo S40, parked just a few streets away.

He sends a coded text message to an emergency number. If this thing's planned for tomorrow, they've got to get moving now. He can give them the details later.

He steps back a little, as much to escape the stench of his dying informant's excrement as to survey the immediate vicinity of the wrecked bar.

It's a good job Inspector Mokrane Méguelati does that.

A second team.

There's a second team.

A metallic brown Series 1 BMW, rifle muzzles protruding out of the rear window as it slows down outside the Bar de l'Amitié.

Inspector Mokrane Méguelati realises he's a sitting duck, standing there alone amid all the wreckage.

The shooting's already begun.

Inspector Mokrane Méguelati is convinced the hail of bullets is going to cut him in half. Bizarrely, the bullets miss him, except for one which destroys his smartphone. He crawls along the floor, gun in hand, makes it to the very back of the bar, sees the toilet, crawls through the door, locks it behind him.

Another burst of bullets rattles the door. Broken bits of wood everywhere. A window high up in the wall for him to escape through. The flawless leap. Running through the streets of Saint-François Hill. They can't go on chasing him forever, the fucking *schbebs*. That now makes two profanities in the same evening. Inspector Mokrane Méguelati hasn't sworn this much since he was a teenager.

Smoking gun in hand, breathing steadily like the marathon runner he is, he looks over his shoulder from time to time. Where the hell are his colleagues? Despite what those neo-reactionary intellectuals would have you believe, a shooting with Kalashnikovs, even in The 800 – well it's not something that happens every day.

He eventually reaches a street that's a little bit busier, the rue Jean-Pierre-Stirbois (formerly the rue Emile-Pouget).

Inspector Mokrane Méguelati sees a navy blue Duster moving slowly towards him. Idiots from the Municipal Police. Still, that's better than nothing, especially if those Islamists show up. Those idiots from the Municipal Police now have firepower worthy of a western military coalition in a Middle Eastern desert, ever since the new mayor decided he needed a Pretorian Guard (a useful status symbol, and a way of signalling just how seriously he takes public safety around here).

Inspector Mokrane Méguelati starts gesticulating

frantically with the Glock 41 he's holding in his right hand. One of the officers steps out of the Duster. He's carrying a riot gun. And Inspector Mokrane Méguelati is both astonished and horrified when the officer shoots him full in the face and kills him, leaving nothing in his wake but a little gun smoke and the handful of images that flash before the eyes of the dying man: Fadila's breasts in the bathroom of a hotel in Saint-Malo last spring; little girls' toys strewn across the back seat of his Volvo C40; the pencil nestling behind his dad's ear; and the sound of the sea as it ebbs and flows across the pebbles on the beach.

4

And there we must bid farewell to Inspector Mokrane Méguelati. It's a shame really. He was a nice guy. For a cop. The reader may be interested to know that his widow, Fadila Méguelati, and his two daughters, Warda and Juliette, will soon leave this port city in the West. Fadila, driven by a desire for vengeance which will prevent her from being consumed by grief, will embark upon a reasonably successful career in banking. She will contact the colleagues of her deceased husband, and will offer to work for them. She will prove to be a very useful ally in their fight against the funding of terrorism. She will earn the admiration of experts in this field by finding all sorts of complex, twisted ways of persuading the ruling families of oil-rich emirates, known for their duplicitous habit of officially supporting the West while unofficially siding with the leaders of the Islamic world, to pour their money into risky investment schemes. She will find some consolation in the knowledge that her actions have left these families financially crippled, thereby forcing them to sell at knock-down prices their yachts moored off the Côte d'Azur, their manor houses in the Chevreuse valley and their football clubs riding high at the top of the various European leagues.

5

The coded text message sent by the late Inspector Méguelati reaches its destination, even though his smartphone is destroyed. It sends shockwaves throughout the French Directorate for Internal Security on this June evening. It also mobilises the truly remarkable number of police officers and gendarmes who patrol The 800 every night.

Usually, it's just the guys from the Serious Crimes Squad who come to play what the technocrats refer to as their *proactive role* or, if you prefer, come to provoke the locals – anything to help inflate those crime statistics: spot-checking ID; provoking fatal accidents by giving chase to kids on scooters; bursting Clint Eastwood-like into thc graffiti-covered entrances to tower blocks where drug dealing's going on. The dealers point out to them, before being gently manhandled, that it's really quite astonishing, the way they're being prevented from playing their part in the market economy when the experts on TV keep insisting that nothing should stand in the way of free trade, especially not archaic laws that have failed to keep up with the way society has evolved. Or words to that effect.

But this time, we're talking about a colleague killed in cold blood who managed to warn them that there's something nasty afoot, along with four corpses in a bar, including a couple of bearded blokes with Kalashnikovs and the colleague's informant. Not to mention the fact that, according to witnesses, there's a second team of two or three gunmen out there somewhere.

Not good.

So, in The 800 and throughout the rest of this large port city in the West, in the middle of the night, thanks to the powers granted to them by the State of Emergency, the police undertake a massive search operation. A Special Firearms team is called in, known terrorist suspects are arrested, and while they're about it, the police also evict the residents of an anarchists' squat that's been holding up a building project in the Jeanval area of the city. Despite their best efforts, they find nothing and the next day is edging dangerously closer. They smash doors in – and skulls too – and shout a lot, drive around with their sirens wailing, they piss everybody off until, naturally enough, they provoke a riot.

It's a tough job, maintaining law and order – no two ways about it.

And somewhere in Paris – avenue de Villiers, Levallois, to be precise - in the bowels of the high-security building occupied by the French Directorate for Internal Security, at three o'clock in the morning, a senior official is screaming down his telephone at the Interior Minister's Chief of Staff. The senior official – a bastard, but a competent bastard – is explaining that responding to an imminent terrorist threat by kicking up such a rumpus is bloody stupid. That there's a fucking communication problem between the different departments, that this isn't the first time this kind of thing has happened, and that it's just about gone far enough, for Christ's sake.

The Interior Minister's Chief of Staff, a man in his thirties with an impeccable career record thus far, asks himself, as he looks at his pretty wife snoring gently there in bed next to him thanks to the three sleeping pills she took earlier, whether he wouldn't have been better off supporting Durieux, the Education Minister, rather than Bastiani, Interior Minister, if he really wanted to be given a chance of a seat for the party at the next General Election . True, teachers are a pain in the arse, but they're not half as bad as the boys from the Interior Ministry, who despise each other even more than if they'd graduated together from the École Nationale d'Administration.

6

The reason for all this, the Combatant, lying in hiding at the back of a cellar in a block of flats in the bowels of The 800, looks at his watch and sees that it's now 03.50. But of course it has to do, once again, with distant geopolitical conflicts that have found their way here, in this port city in the West.

The Combatant thinks the operation is fucked.

He wants a cigarette, but the smoke might attract the attention of the cops who continue to go through The 800 with a fine-tooth comb while the riot, up there at street level, approaches its orgiastic climax. The Combatant hates himself for making that kind of comparison.

It's all that Little Rebel's fault, she's got under his skin. The Combatant loves her blond hair, her unshaven cunt which smells of seawater, like the white caves under the cliffs of Jeanval. That's where he made love to the Little Rebel for the first time. It was dangerous, because of the risk of a landslip, and the rising tide.

But there was that skin of hers, her mouth so hot around his cock, the smell of seaweed, salt and iodine. It was the Little Rebel who had chosen that spot. The Little Rebel was strange. She hadn't said a word, merely stuck a finger up his arsehole. The Combatant was ashamed of himself. He had nearly hit her. And yet he had loved it and had come like never before.

Thinking about it all now, the Combatant gets a hard-on.

The idea of radicalising the Little Rebel had occurred to him in a flash. The Little Rebel never said yes, or no, to anything. The Little Rebel was always calm, indifferent, she got her kicks in silence. The Little Rebel was beautiful but inconspicuous. She knew how to make herself invisible. The Little Rebel spent her days reading anything and everything. Even in high school, she was inconspicuous. Her grades were average, and she didn't hang around with any particular group of kids.

The Combatant realised pretty quickly that the Little Rebel didn't give a shit about religion. The Little Rebel didn't give a shit about anything. The Little Rebel didn't hang out with anybody, except one or two boys, sometimes. The Little Rebel had a few girlfriends but no real friends and didn't even have a Facebook page.

And yet the Little Rebel listened to what the Combatant had to say. On one occasion, the Little Rebel had just said, 'I'm fine with the idea of blowing the world sky-high, but don't give me any of your bullshit. I'll do whatever you want. You have your reasons for hurting people, I have mine. For you it's Allah, for me it's because the world is an ugly place and I find nothing of interest in it.'

The Combatant had been torn between fear and anger, but had quickly snuffed out both of those feelings. The Combatant already had his plan, his idea on how to use the Little Rebel and then get rid of her. He had understood, thanks to his conversation with the Imam, that the Little Rebel embodied the essence of evil, the very heart of darkness, but the Imam had told him that Jihad could make use of evil to achieve its goals.

From his bunker, the Combatant can hear a helicopter flying over the tower blocks just like in Afghanistan, or Syria, or Libya. The Combatant doesn't need to see it to know what it looks like, up there in the sky.

The 800 is where he spent his youth. And his youth was one riot after another. A dress rehearsal for war, especially the riots in 2005, when The 800 was up in flames, when they even managed to burn down half the lycée Tillon, where the Combatant was marking time learning how to be a mechanic (*motorcycle maintenance* as the French call it, in their eternally duplicitous language).

He lights a cigarette. Might as well now.

The Combatant has made a mistake, and he knows it.

An entire network wiped out, all because of Abdul and that bastard cop who was always following him around everywhere. The Combatant had believed he was in a war zone, had thought that he could behave like they did over there, that shooting indiscriminately would be enough to salvage an operation.

The Combatant knows that the trail will lead back to him, sooner rather than later.

For a long time, the Combatant had obeyed the Imam's instructions and concealed his desire to strike down the infidels who treated him, his parents and his grandparents like second-class French citizens. The Imam had told him, 'Stay in the shadows, do not reveal your Faith even if you wish to do so. The infidels are watching us, so you must live like them. Be sure to have a drink now and again, wear the clothes they wear. You will be of far better use to us that way, and those who need to know will indeed know that you are truly on our side, I will make sure of that.'

So the Combatant hadn't grown a beard, nor had he tried to radicalise his colleagues at the Manzoni garage where he worked.

The Imam's connections were good, and the Combatant had been able to train and kill in the name of Islam during his summer holidays. Each time he returned to work at the Manzoni garage, pulled on his overalls, and carried out his MOTs, his workmates would talk about their camping holiday in the south of France, their evenings spent out clubbing, or their fishing trips. He would reply that he'd also had a good vacation, back in his native village somewhere in the Maghreb, while all the time the stench of death would be as fresh in his nostrils as the images were vivid in his mind's eye: the desert sun, the white-walled ruins in the villages, the charred remains of tanks littering the crossroads, the faceless corpses, prayers recited amid the reek of sweat and carnage.

The Combatant would look at his colleagues and say to himself, 'It'll be your turn soon.'

And last month, the Combatant had told the Little Rebel what he expected of her after they'd made love, as they always did, in the cave under the cliffs at Jeanval.

The Little Rebel had said yes with those eyes of hers that were so blue, and so empty. The Combatant had outlined his idea to the Imam. They'd discussed it with the others at the mosque, Rue Aristote. They'd added the finishing touches to the plan. The Little Rebel was above suspicion. The Little Rebel would know exactly what to do. The Combatant had shown her, in between fucks. They'd dropped the equipment off at her place. It was perfectly safe; the Little Rebel lived alone in a two-bedroom flat in a tower block with her mother who was doped up to her eyeballs on antidepressants.

'I want you to drive the Little Rebel to the location, but then you've got to get straight out of there', 'I want you to wait there until the bomb's gone off', 'I want you to make the phone call to claim responsibility.' It was early evening, just as they were discussing the finer details with the rest of the group in the premises of their Youth Club near the Rue Aristote mosque, when the Combatant and the Imam had noticed the presence of Abdul Slimane in the next room, watching television.

Impossible to know exactly what Slimane had heard. But they couldn't take the risk, they couldn't trust him, especially since he'd left the premises sharpish, looking very shifty. The dirty little dope-peddling junkie.

'Deal with it,' the Imam told the Combatant.

And he had obeyed.

But nothing had gone according to plan. The carnage at the Bar de l'Amitié. The dead cop. Abdul Slimane had a rendezvous with a cop. It must have been a cop, given the way the fella had dealt with the first team. Slimane was almost certainly an informant, as certain members in the group had begun to suspect. Like that cop, Slimane was a bastard who had betrayed Jihad. Birds of a feather...

It's fucked. I'm fucked. The operation's fucked, the Combatant thinks to himself, stubbing out his cigarette on what's left of his coffee, lying there stuck to the bottom of his glass.

Unless.

Unless the Little Rebel does something unexpected.

After all, you never know.

The Little Rebel is so... inconspicuous.

Apart from when she's in those caves at Jeanval, where her body really feels like a body. A body the Combatant would certainly miss. The Combatant won't find another one like it this side of Paradise. He doubts the virgins waiting for him up there stick their fingers up your arse.

Even now, the Combatant can see the cops breaking down the reinforced door of their hideout.

He mumbles a prayer, but, truth be told, he always gets a hard-on when he imagines himself squeezing the trigger of the Kalashnikov he took last summer from the corpse of an officer in the Syrian army in a suburb of Alep. He screams his head off as he fires round after round into the first Robocop from the Special Firearms team that breaks into his hideout.

7

Two hundred and eighty kilometres away, Alizé Lavaux wakes up at 5am with a hangover, in a ridiculously small and incredibly expensive flat in the Rue Pétion, in the eleventh arrondissement of Paris. She drank too many shots of vodka in a bar in the city's Oberkampf district last night. And if Alizé Lavaux drank too many shots of vodka, it's because Alizé Lavaux is going to leave the part-time actor who's still asleep in the same bed, even though he's cute, at least according to the fashion of the day, which means he's a bit of a weed and his chin's covered in designer stubble.

He's perfect, he's good in bed, they see eye to eye on everything, and what's more, he's ten years younger than Alizé Lavaux, who has just turned thirty-nine. But Alizé Lavaux doesn't love him any longer. You see, Alizé Lavaux is mistaking love for passion. Alizé Lavaux has already been told by certain people who used to be her friends – but who aren't anymore – that she's nothing more than a postmodern kind of Emma Bovary.

Alizé Lavaux walks into the bathroom.

'For a girl who's about to hit forty and who's had four hours' sleep after a night spent boozing and smoking two or three joints, you're not looking too bad,' Alizé tells her reflection in the mirror.

She has a point.

She's quite a Pretty Polly, with her short ginger hair and green eyes tainted by nothing but the merest hint of crow's feet. Alizé Lavaux asks herself – silently this time, as she has no desire to disturb the part-time actor who is for now on reprieve after that awkward discussion in the bar in Oberkampf, a discussion which ended more or less at the same time that Inspector Mokrane Méguelati was playing Davy Crockett in another bar where shots of vodka don't cost quite as much as a trolley-load of shopping in a discount supermarket – so Alizé Lavaux asks herself whether her miraculously youthful appearance, her silhouette worthy of a teenage girl in a manga, doesn't have something to do with her job: she writes stories for children and a group of people referred to these days as *young adults*.

Alizé Lavaux has written stories for tiny tots, 6-9-year-olds, 9-12-year-olds, 12-15-year-olds, and the aforementioned *young adults*. Some of her books have been very successful, such as *The Little Bear Who Couldn't Ride a Bike* (for the tiny tots), *Teacher Just Got Divorced* (for the 6-9-year-olds), *A Martian in the Fridge* (for the 9-12-year-olds), *The Boy Who Liked Boys* (for the 12-15-year-olds) and *Redundancy Plan* (for the *young adults*).

Alizé Lavaux is one of those writers for children who makes a living out of writing, what with her book sales, her writing workshops, and the seminars she runs in schools. She is regarded by her colleagues as a serious girl, 'nice' and quite talented – a reasonably accurate description. Alizé Lavaux generally avoids tub-thumping or voyeurism in her books, and she does not go out of her way to 'challenge' the beliefs of her young readers. Alizé Lavaux, with some justification, that the world is sufficiently challenging as it is – and 'challenged' – thank you very much.

Alizé Lavaux steps out of the shower and into clothes which she had picked out last night, while still just about lucid. This avoids the usual rummaging around in her wardrobe which would only disturb her future ex-boyfriend.

Alizé Lavaux is due to speak at 9am to a Lower Sixth class specialising in Sales, Negotiation, and Customer Management and Retention at a vocational and technical lycée situated in a port city in the West. She has therefore chosen a noncommittal kind of outfit: a pair of jeans that aren't too tight, a plain blue t-shirt, and a beige linen blouse to match her Converse sneakers. This way she avoids looking either too sexy (the kind of look she opts for when she wants to provoke people in private Catholic high schools), or too rock 'n' roll (her go-to style for getting up the noses of people in the posher state-run establishments).

According to the emails she's received and what she's been told on the phone by the school's librarian and its French teacher, who have invited her to talk about her most recent novel for 'young adults', an anti-capitalist dystopia entitled *Sun for Everyone!*, today's lycée is 'a difficult establishment, but whose pupils are keen to have their intellectual horizons expanded'. This means (for Alizé Lavaux has learnt to see through the hot air spouted by education spin doctors) that this school is in a rough part of town, and is little more than a dumping ground for testosterone-fuelled hoodlums and girls whose dress sense fluctuates between a kind of crypto-Muslim style, a dumb-blond look, and shapeless sweatpants designed to help them blend into the background.

The part-time actor who's nearly thirty slowly wakes as Alizé is putting the finishing touches to her make-up by the mirror hanging on the back of the front door.

'Can we have a talk when you get back tonight?' he mumbles plaintively, slurring his words a little.

'Yeah, sure.'

'Do you love me?'

Alizé Lavaux pretends she hasn't heard this last question, picks up her bag and, half an hour later, drinks a coffee at the gare Saint-Lazare, while flicking through a free paper with an article entitled 'Allergies: All You Need to Know about the Bug Threat' on its front page.

'Well at least it's not Muslims this time,' Alizé Lavaux mutters to herself, while standing on the platform and rolling the first of her thirty cigarettes of the day, before boarding the train that will take her to the port city in the West.

8

The reason why Flavien Dubourg, who is twenty-seven years old and teaches French at the vocational and technical lycée named after Resistance hero and Communist politician Charles Tillon, is masturbating while thinking of the photos of Alizé Lavaux he found on Google is to be found in the quite depressing sexual mores characteristic of the times in which we live.

Flavien Dubourg is still a virgin, and this is really getting him down. He isn't that bad looking really – well, no worse than anybody else. In fact, he looks a bit like Alizé Lavaux's actor, only less of a hipster. For one thing, he has practically no facial hair to speak of, so he'd have trouble with the old designer stubble. But he's auburn-haired, with a nice face, a friendly smile and a calm voice, and he usually wears tweed or linen jackets and chinos. Although, at the moment he's lying naked in bed with his dick in his hand, imagining Alizé Lavaux straddling him. She pinches his nipples, whispers obscenities in his ear and gives him a slap when he comes.

There we are... Now he's finished, Flavien Dubourg feels sticky but contented under the damp sheets. Flavien Dubourg will have to go to the launderette, instead of asking his mother to wash the sheets with the rest of his stuff, which he does every Saturday when he has dinner with his parents. They are retired Post Office workers, and live in a renovated farmhouse on the edge of a village near the port city in the West.

Flavien Dubourg is, despite everything, quite lucid when it comes to the reasons behind his depressing sex life. However, just because he understands the why doesn't make the what any less depressing. Flavien Dubourg has grown up in a society notable for its schizophrenia. This society overexposes its citizens to a pornographic version of sex on the internet, and he's pretty sure he saw his first online double penetration when he was thirteen. On the other hand, these days the most innocent attempt at flirting with a colleague is likely to land the perpetrator in court, on a charge of sexual harassment.

Bit of a problem really.

During those few encounters he's had with women he's been incapable of getting it up, even with one of the working girls down by the docks renowned for her patience. Flavien Dubourg has consulted a doctor about his problem – although not the Dubourg family doctor – and that doctor told him, after sending him to several specialists, that his problem is purely psychological, and that he is not the only heterosexual male to suffer from this affliction.

Flavien has also observed the havoc wreaked by pornography among the pupils of Charles-Tillon. But ultimately Flavien Dubourg, whose CV includes ideas close to those held by many on the radical left, alongside the teaching of French and history, cannot find it in him to condemn these young people. It has to be said though, that by the way they look to a fucking stupid religion to tell them who they are (although all religions are fucking stupid, as he's always quick to tell himself), these boys leave the girls with a very stark choice: they can either be whore or slave, to paraphrase the famous head of a charity organisation who enjoyed a very brief career as a government minister under Sarkozy.

All the effort Flavien Dubourg puts into planning his lessons won't make a blind bit of difference. Back in the real world, however, his pubes are now encrusted with dry cum, so if he doesn't want to be late to welcome Alizé Lavaux to the school, he'd better get a move on.

Flavien Dubourg is feeling a bit nervous though. His Lower Sixth class aren't wild about *Sun for Everyone!* and the school librarian is even more pessimistic: 'I don't know why you waste your time with that lot, they couldn't give a shit. Apart from Stacy Billon who's read the whole novel, the others are just going to ask stupid questions – that's assuming that they don't start a riot. I know you're going to say that these kids are entitled to have access to culture, that these young people, most of whom are heading for a job in telesales, will be interested to read a novel like this which critiques the whole consumer culture thing, but you know as well as I do that it's just not going to happen.'

The librarian has one more year to go before retirement. She often talks about her rebellious youth back in the seventies, but Flavien thinks old age hasn't been very kind to her.

A few months ago, sitting down at the librarian's desk to check a list of pupils registered for a reading group on her computer, Flavien Dubourg came across the woman's browsing history and saw that she regularly consulted the websites of extreme right-wing groups, which mostly consisted of articles about how, now the Muslims had taken over, the tower blocks had become no-go areas, the White Man was no longer free to do as he pleased in his own back yard, the principle of non-religious education was under attack on a daily basis etc., etc.

Flavien Dubourg was so shocked that he wondered whether the librarian hadn't voted for the victorious Patriotic Bloc in the last municipal elections. After all, the 37% of the vote they scored in the first round, and their 44% in the three-way split in the second round, must have come from somewhere. But still, for a woman who used to be on the extreme left…

Flavien Dubourg didn't say anything. After all, he had his own little secret, which although perhaps not quite so dirty, is shocking nevertheless: his decision to invite Alizé Lavaux rather than any other writer has more to do with her physical charms than with any passion Flavien Dubourg might feel for *Sun for Everyone!*

He has already invited a number of other young people's writers to his school. One of them recommended to him the work of Alizé Lavaux, which Flavien Dubourg hadn't read at the time.

When Flavien Dubourg, thinking about that conversation a few weeks later, Googled pictures of the author, it was love at first sight. Alizé Lavaux was exactly the kind of redhead who drove Flavien Dubourg crazy, reminding him of Marlène Jobert.

One of his very first masturbatory fantasies as a teenager had involved the freckle-faced Jobert stepping out of the shower holding a pistol in her hand, when he'd come across *Police War* on one of his dad's old video tapes. He found this image more memorable than all the acrobatics actors get up to on internet porn sites, which suggests that Flavien Dubourg is not just a virgin who likes a wank, but a virgin who likes an intellectual kind of wank.

Which is why, on this sunny June morning, Flavien Dubourg turns the ignition key in his old second-hand Renault Clio and listens to a Manu Chao CD rather than the news as he drives to work at the Charles-Tillon lycée.

Flavien Dubourg is all hot and bothered at the thought of his forthcoming meeting with Alizé Lavaux. He barely notices the heightened police presence. Despite his extreme-left views, he forgets to moan when traffic begins to slow after the Allied Forces roundabout, and Flavien Dubourg waves his ID absentmindedly at a cop on a motorbike before setting off again.

On the train to the port city in the West, Alizé Lavaux is sitting in a practically empty carriage and desperately trying to resist the temptation to smoke. She thinks about her forthcoming meeting with the pupils of the Charles-Tillon lycée, about her actor boyfriend whom she's preparing to ditch, about the fact that she's going to be forty next birthday, and about the hangover she's trying to cure with paracetamol, washed down with all the mineral water she's brought with her. Alizé Lavaux doesn't feel like opening her bag and taking out the manuscript of her latest novel, despite the fact that she's promised herself she'll make some edits during the journey.

9

The Charles-Tillon vocational and technical lycée is located in the southern area of the city. It was put up in a hurried, slapdash manner, during the real estate boom of the early 70s. Nearly 45 years later, the Regional Council has finally come up with the money, and Charles-Tillon is no longer falling to pieces but is in fact currently being completely rebuilt. It resembles something of a construction site, in which new buildings, thrown up just as quickly and badly as in the 70s but this time with environmental norms firmly in mind – which changes everything – are gradually replacing the old ones. Meanwhile, classes continue in prefab huts strewn across patches of wasteland, all of which reinforces the sinister air of the place, stuck as it is on the edge of the city, near the dual carriageway leading to the motorway for Paris, at the bottom of a ridge formed by a gigantic retail park where a number of the school's pupils find their internships.

It's sad, notes Flavien Dubourg as he parks his Clio in the car park reserved for the lycée's teaching staff, which can only be accessed via a magnetic card, to think that even though the sea is really close, there's nowhere in Charles-Tillon where one can actually see it. Flavien Dubourg likes to imagine that a view of the sea would help the pupils relax, that it would enable them to dream, to feel noble feelings.

Flavien Dubourg often thinks like this. He is two hundred years ahead of his time. He is a denizen of the world to come, a golden age in which, once our technocratic, consumerist society has collapsed, we will all live in harmony with each other in the trees, and will spend our days reading poetry. This will be a land of milk and honey, a place from which work, capitalism, lycées under reconstruction, shopping centres and bad sex will be forever banished. Meanwhile, Flavien Dubourg has to elbow his way through a crowd of students.

As he does so, he wonders how his Lower Sixth Sales class will react to *Sun for Everyone!*, whether Alizé Lavaux will accept his invitation to lunch in a brasserie near the station when he gives her a lift in his Clio later on, whether the pubes of this children's author are as ginger as the rest of her hair – if indeed she still has pubes, given the current appalling fashion for shaving off all one's body hair... He is so lost in thought, that he fails to notice there are rather fewer students around than normal, and less commotion in the playground, and that the students who are there seem quite preoccupied and are talking in rather more hushed tones than usual, huddled together under the cloudless blue sky on this already hot morning.

Flavien Dubourg makes his way towards the part of Charles-Tillon where the rebuilding work has already finished, which houses the school's administration, the library and the staff room. As he enters the building the Deputy Head, a man who has managed to retain his almost preternatural composure in spite of the post he occupies and the challenging environment, brings him up to speed with the previous night's events.

'A riot, Mr Dubourg, over at The 800. Following a shooting in a bar. The whole city's talking about it! And it looks like quite a few pupils have stayed home this morning. I sent somebody to pick Mme Lavaux from the station as arranged, but I'm afraid your class will be far from full. But there she is now!'

Alizé Lavaux appears, her bag slung over her shoulder. No doubt about it – Alizé Lavaux is sexy. Even the male students who are busy swapping rumours and information while waiting for the 9 o'clock bell to ring stop for a second to take a look at this elf-like ginger-haired woman as she arrives at the school on this sunny June morning.

Alizé Lavaux is wearing a rather forced smile. Alizé Lavaux had time, while waiting to be picked up from the station, to read the Breaking News alerts on her Samsung. She thinks it's just her bloody luck. A city under siege.

She has also had the time to smoke two roll-ups before spotting the man sent to pick her up, holding up a piece of cardboard with 'Alizé Lavaux' written on it. Alizé Lavaux has booked a return on the 13.47 train and, although she realises this is rather unsociable of her, is nevertheless keeping everything crossed that she makes it. When it comes to urban revolt, of course she unfailingly sides with those doing the revolting, but she prefers them not to choose places where she's appearing, especially if her love life happens to be going through a rough patch at the same time.

Flavien Dubourg feels his heart flutter. He tries to forget those images from his morning wank and forces himself to be professional and charming, even though the palms of his hands feel damp and a trickle of sweat runs down his back.

'Hello, I'm Flavien Dubourg, and this is our Deputy Head. Thank you for accepting the invitation that my colleague the librarian and I sent you. Things are a little tense this morning. I'm sure you've heard about what happened here last night. But I'm sure we'll have a very fruitful seminar, nevertheless. Writers such as Sébastien Gendron and Dominique Forma have told me about the excellent rapport you have with students. Why don't we go and have a coffee in the library before the class joins us there?'

The Deputy Head clears his throat a little, which is his particular way of expressing extreme embarrassment.

'There's another problem, M. Dubourg. But allow me, Mme Lavaux, to say just how delighted I am to meet you, and to thank you for agreeing to come and meet our students. I was just about to let M. Dubourg know that it won't be possible to have your seminar in the library. The librarian is off sick today. A very bad migraine apparently...'

The bitch, thinks Flavien Dubourg, feeling his legs begin to shake. There are numerous copies of *Sun for Everyone!* in the library, along with a display of students' work on the novel, alternative book covers, press articles dealing with some of the issues raised in the book, etc. The students would normally have their copies of the novel with them, as well as some prepared questions to ask the author, but Flavien Dubourg knows that it's always a good idea to use the library, just in case.

'I'm sure there must be a spare set of keys to the place somewhere!' Flavien Dubourg says, trying to control his feeling of panic at the prospect of the forthcoming lesson-from-hell. Not to mention the fact that if the seminar is a disaster, he can kiss goodbye to his idea of inviting Alizé Lavaux to lunch in the brasserie near the station, and all he'll have to look forward to tonight will be yet another date with Miss W. Rist.

'There should be, yes,' says the Deputy Head. 'But we don't seem to be able to find them. Your colleague the librarian must have both sets of keys with her. And our Head of Works doesn't have the passes for the new buildings; we had to return them all to the manufacturer yesterday as they were faulty. What with all the rebuilding going on and last night's events, we're a little overstretched, to be honest. We're trying to work out how many students are missing after what happened last night so that we can let the Local Education Authority know, the police have just asked us to check everybody entering and leaving the premises, our Headmaster has gone to a crisis meeting with other heads in the city, and we have had two fights break out among our Sixth Form Dry Cleaning students, no doubt due to an argument about last night's events. One boy has suffered severe burns after being attacked with an iron, and a girl has had stain remover thrown in her eyes. They're in the infirmary. We're expecting an ambulance to arrive any moment now.'

The Deputy Head serves up this apocalyptic description of

the morning's events in a voice that is at once measured and barely audible, as the commotion among the students gets louder and louder, the closer it gets to 9 o'clock.

Flavien Dubourg suddenly has a vision: it's as if he can see right through the Deputy Head's body, can see the man's blood vessels carrying those antidepressants up towards his brain. Flavien Dubourg realises that for all his apparent British-style sang-froid, the man has to be practically brain-dead.

'What are we going to do then? I've arranged to meet the students by the library. They'll be there any minute now.'

'Don't fret, M. Dubourg!'

That's easy to say when you're doped up to the eyeballs on Anafranil, Seroxat and Fluoxetine – or very probably all three at once.

'I'm not fretting. I'm merely trying to ensure that Mme Lavaux's meeting with the students goes as well as possible.'

'Why don't you both go on ahead to your prefab... er, your temporary classroom. I'll get somebody to bring the students along. As I say, I doubt very much you'll have a full class today. That classroom should be more than adequate, don't you think?'

Flavien Dubourg crosses his fingers that at least Stacy Billon will be there. He knows he can count on her. Stacy Billon won't let him down; she's bound to have her copy of the book with her and her list of questions.

'I hope that will be OK with you, Mme Lavaux,' says the Deputy Head, whom Flavien Dubourg can still see through, his luminescent body bathed in a silver glow, thanks to all those serotonin uptake inhibitors swimming around inside it.

Alizé Lavaux acquiesces impassively. She seems rather distracted, blasé even. In actual fact, Alizé Lavaux is wondering what the fuck she's doing here for the 226 euros after tax that she'll get in three months' time, and (in no particular order of importance) whether she'll make that 13.47 train, whether she should really leave her part-time actor after all, whether this Flavien Dubourg always dresses like Philippe Noiret playing some lord of the manor, or if he's made a special effort for her, whether or not she might have time to roll herself another ciggy – just a quick one – and whether she's remembered to put a packet of mints in her bag because she thinks she smells like a vodka distillery and she must have donkey's breath. Vodka, yuk, at her age, the night before meeting a group of school kids, bloody stupid idea, is what she's thinking, this Alizé Lavaux.

10

Flavien Dubourg walks with Alizé Lavaux through the grounds of the school-cum-building site towards the prefabricated hut that has been his classroom for several months, located some distance away on what will one day be Charles-Tillon's new playground but which for now is a patch of wasteland. Fortunately, the sun's out and it's already warm even though it's not yet 9 o'clock; heat and dust are always nicer than mud and drizzle.

'I feel like a smoke,' says Alizé Lavaux. In theory this is forbidden. The librarian, had she graced them with her presence – the bloody closet fascist – would have gone so far as to say that smokers get picked on far too easily in this school – certainly a lot more easily than those lads who've swapped their Snoop Dogg look for the *nice believer* outfit, complete with white djellaba, little hat and straggly beard, or those girls who wear long brown skirts as if they were nuns. 'What's the bloody point me sticking the Charter for Non-Religious Education up all over the place?' the librarian often asks straight out, when she's having a quick fag by the little window of the library's kitchenette at break-time.

Flavien Dubourg, motivated as much by an absence of Islamophobic paranoia as by the sex mania which drives him to ogle discreetly the tight, round little asses of the girls in his lycée, would be more likely to point to the number of denim mini-skirts on parade at Charles-Tillon, and give thanks for the fact that the nice weather has brought his students to their fashion senses.

'Just a quick one, then...' Flavien Dubourg replies to Alizé Lavaux with a smile. 'I know, it's a bit stupid, given that we're in the middle of a building site, but you know the rule on school premises...'

Flavien Dubourg nurtures the rather pathetic hope that his answer will help him curry favour with Alizé Lavaux. Permission granted, Alizé Lavaux rolls herself a cigarette with incredible dexterity and rapidity, without breaking her stride, and smokes it behind the prefab hut just as the school bell strikes 9 o'clock.

When she reappears, sucking a mint which she's managed to find at the bottom of her bag, the students are there accompanied by a teaching assistant. There's eleven of them out of twenty-seven – and not necessarily the pick of the bunch. Flavien spots Stacy Billon and breathes a sigh of relief. But he also spots Omar Diop, a Senegalese troublemaker who's probably only here because he fancies the little Billon girl, and Quoc Han, who's a reasonably good student, but who's inconsolable since Stacy's stopped looking at him and who's nearly come to blows with Omar on two or three occasions.

'Morning, M. Dubourg! You seen The 800? Bloody mayhem!'

'It's mayhem everywhere, anyway,' Omar Diop says philosophically. 'So you're the author then? It's brill, your book!'

'You haven't even read it,' says Quoc Han. 'You never read anything. I bet you can't even remember the title.'

'Sod off, you jerk. We haven't even sat down yet and you're already starting to get on my tits.'

'Cut it out, you two! Let's all go inside. We can discuss things in there,' says Flavien Dubourg.

'Weren't we supposed to be in the library?'

'Change of plans,' says Flavien Dubourg. 'Something to do with the building work that's going on.'

'What did I tell you? Mayhem everywhere!' says Omar Diop. 'Even here at Tillon...'

Alizé Lavaux has got a hold of herself again: last night's vodka has stopped repeating on her, and that ciggy's done her the world of good. Alizé Lavaux assumes her role. As the students go into the prefab hut, Alizé Lavaux steps aside to let the huge Omar pass, and smiles as she says to him, 'If by any chance you haven't read my book yet, I hope to convince you that it's worth reading.'

Omar smiles a big, almost soft smile. Omar often looks as though he were ten, rather than twice that age. He finds Alizé Lavaux sexy and sweet at the same time. The combination confuses him for a second. He doesn't want to conjure up the kinds of images that would dishonour Alizé Lavaux, as he regularly does with Stacy Billon. That same Stacy Billon who he didn't even manage to shag when the two of them did their internship with the same telesales company. Stacy has a boyfriend in The 800, where she lives, apparently. Omar lives in another part of town, otherwise it would have happened by now. She might look like a bluestocking, but she's a real goer, that Stacy Billon, if rumours are to be believed.

As the students take their seats in the prefab hut, Flavien Dubourg thinks there's no way he's going to make the seminar drag on until midday without the pre-prepared questions and the copies of the book.

What's more, Flavien Dubourg is a little mad at Omar. Flavien Dubourg imagines the Senegalese kid giving Alizé Lavaux a fantastic orgasm. *I'm getting bogged down in racist stereotypes*, he thinks, *but for Christ's sake why have I never had a shag while that thick black kid over there probably gets his bloody leg over every other day*?

All of which goes to show that the emancipatory ideas of the radical left are as nothing when compared to the weight of sexual frustration and that if only we'd listened to Wilhelm Reich's ideas on the sexual revolution instead of putting him in prison, we'd no doubt be much better off.

11

The reason why, at about five minutes past nine, ten or so individuals, some in uniform, others in civilian clothes, are gathered around a dreary-looking table in a room filled with the kind of plain and simple, grey and beige furniture beloved of all presidential administrations, including the administration dedicated to fighting the war against terrorism, can be found in the way in which distant geopolitical conflicts last night took on a very concrete form in the port city in the West: shootings, rioting, and the specific, imminent threat of a terrorist attack.

The men and the one woman around the table lean frequently over the iPads in front of them. They haven't had much sleep. The room smells of coffee and aftershave. A senior police officer feels himself sweating. The senior officer is overweight, it's hot outside and there's no air con in here.

'We know that the Imam, the Combatant and their men have been neutralised.'

'And there are only a few handfuls of rioters left.'

'You will agree that it would have been better to capture the man called the Combatant alive. We could have got him to talk.'

'May I remind you that the Combatant killed a guy from the Special Firearms Unit, and wounded two others. If you thought you could do better, why didn't you send your own men in?'

'I agree. We managed to dismantle an entire local cell that

was about to carry out an attack – and in the middle of a riot as well. I don't think we did too badly really.'

'Is that so? But what if the attack hasn't been called off after all, what if it's going ahead as planned? If that happens, we could all still end up with egg on our faces.'

'Lady and gentlemen, let's not get carried away here. What exactly do we know? We've accounted for every last one of the bastards, haven't we?'

'All except for two men, possibly three,' says the only female member of the group, a rather strict-looking woman in her fifties who was recently appointed local Director for Public Safety.

'Who are they?'

'The guys in the second team at the Bar de l'Amitié.'

'Bit of a problem, that.'

'Isn't it just? They're out there somewhere, armed with Kalashnikovs, maybe grenades too.'

'I have a possible ID. At least for two of them. We'll get them soon enough. Their IDs have been sent to all relevant personnel,' says a man in civilian clothes who is none other than the Head of the French Directorate for Internal Security, the man who just a few hours earlier had the argument with the Interior Minister's Chief of Staff.

'I have that information too,' replies the local Director for Public Safety, a little impatiently. She helps herself to another coffee, thinking about adding some artificial sweetener before eventually deciding against it. 'But in for a penny, in for a pound – they may very well decide to commit some kind of atrocity in the city centre, shooting at random into a crowd. Café terraces, the railway station, a school… They're not exactly short on ideas, these nutters, especially now they're dead men walking.'

The local Director for Public Safety slides a finger across the screen of her iPad.

'For example, one of the two men identified appears to have been expelled from his lycée, three years ago. He went to the same lycée as the Combatant and was there at the same time, two years below. He could perfectly well decide to attack that place... Let's see, it's... Charles-Tillon.'

'Is that the gut feeling of an ex-cop who once had her ear to the ground?' the Head of the French Directorate for Internal Security asks amiably, sweating a little more.

'Old habits die hard, Colonel...' replies the local Director for Public Safety, piqued by the Head's clammy obsequiousness into using aphorisms and speaking a trifle bombastically.

'In that case, let's put the Emergency Plan into operation,' says the man chairing the meeting. 'I want all the city's schools to implement the ESSP with immediate effect. Just for starters. And I want those bastards' heads on a plate. Sharpish.'

12

It's twenty past nine in prefab hut no. 47 at Charles-Tillon lycée when the meeting between Alizé Lavaux and Flavien Dubourg's Lower Sixth Sales class finally gets underway. There's a very simple reason for the delay: Flavien Dubourg had the brilliant, if catastrophic, idea of rearranging the tables into a U-shape in order to make the seminar less formal and to enable everyone to take part as much as possible in the discussion of *Sun for Everyone!*

This resulted in pushing and shoving, laughter, chairs being turned upside down on the dirty lino, and a fight between Omar and Quoc Han.

Flavien Dubourg and Alizé Lavaux helped restore order to the teaching space inside the prefab.

They mucked in to help, and in the ensuing melee somebody laid a hand on Alizé Lavaux's arse while she was bending over to move a table.

It couldn't have been Quoc Han or Omar, since they were off to one side, busy exchanging insults like tomcats on heat. Alizé Lavaux is reluctant to make a scene. She hates herself for being reluctant. She hates herself because she's giving in for all the wrong reasons: because she doesn't want to acquire a reputation as a troublesome author. Alizé Lavaux hates herself for excluding the six girls present from her list of likely suspects.

Why shouldn't Alizé Lavaux be the object of some schoolgirl crush? It wouldn't be the first time. Why should the boys have a monopoly on dickheadedness? Alizé Lavaux is actually quite astonished by just how gender-stereotypical her reaction is, she who increasingly believes that gender has nothing to do with sex (cf. *The Boy Who Liked Boys* for 12-15-year-olds). In any case, there could only be five girl suspects, not six. Stacy Billon has spent the whole time near the door, sitting there impassively. Stacy Billon looks as if she's afraid of breaking something, manoeuvring her body rather cautiously under her ample, gaily patterned tunic which clings to her breasts but which conceals the rest of her body and makes her look quite anachronistically like the woman from Jefferson Airplane singing 'White Rabbit'.

On the other hand, what the omniscient narrator can reveal is that her vantage point enabled Stacy Billon to see exactly which despicable individual defiled Alizé Lavaux by grabbing her privates in the midst of the commotion in prefab hut no. 47.

It is none other than Flavien Dubourg, the teacher.

Yes indeed. Flavien Dubourg is blushing, but given how hot it is in there, he's not the only one whose cheeks are red.

Stacy feels an itch in the region of her hips, although that's quite normal. For the time being, now that she's caught Flavien Dubourg red-handed, Stacy Billon tells herself that in the final analysis, whether they be adults, children, poor or rich, the entire human race is made up of nothing but liars, maniacs, psychopaths, would-be assassins.

Stacy Billon could draw up a whole list of them, but it would be so long that it would be exhausting. The sexually frustrated teacher; the young people's writer who preaches equality, human rights, tolerance and feminism but who daren't say anything when a man touches her arse; those idiots Quoc Han and Omar, whom she's tempted to invite to a three-in-a-bed session, just to put a stop to the testosterone-fest that kicks off whenever they see her; the man in charge of electrical goods at the place in the retail park where she's doing her internship, who needs the same pills as her mother just to get through the day; or the Deputy Head who called her into his office the other day to sign her internship contract, and who thought nobody would recognise that crumpled empty box of Prozac lying there in the bin; and all those other people, all of them so vulgar, so ugly on the inside.

Stacy Billon has just turned seventeen, and you have to understand, you're not serious when you're seventeen, just like Rimbaud said, you just see things the way they are. Stacy Billon must be the only one in the whole school who has read Rimbaud – really read him. Teachers included.

Ever since then, Stacy Billon has been looking for her Harar, her very own personal Ethiopia. Well actually, she's found it. It's just that the others don't know it yet.

13

'Does that mean anything to you, Commissioner, rue Jean-Pierre-Stirbois?'

'Nothing at all, Inspector, why?'

'What about rue Emile-Pouget then?'

'No, nothing at all. Have you got a problem with street names or something?'

'It's the same street as a matter of fact. The Patriotic Bloc just renamed it, that's all.'

'Get to the point, Inspector, for Christ's sake! We're all at the end of our tether here.'

'It's the street where an unfortunate incident last night led to the death of Inspector Méguelati.'

'You call that an "unfortunate incident"? A stupid fucking racist city cop murders one of my best men? What about it?'

'Well it so happens that ten minutes ago we got a phone call from a pensioner who lives on the rue Jean-Pierre-Stirbois. Claims to have shot dead a terrorist in his cellar.'

'Is that so?'

'Yes, sir. I thought the old man had probably lost his marbles, but you never know. So, since everybody's on high alert, I sent two officers to investigate.'

'And...?'

'And it seems he was telling the truth. Turns out the chap, a 96-year-old former Legionnaire who served in Indochina, heard a noise early this morning in his cellar. When he went to take a look, armed with his old Mat 49 submachine gun, he came across a bearded bloke hiding down there. The bearded bloke had a Kalashnikov, and he took a shot at the old man, but he missed. The old man made mincemeat out of him. When the Special Firearms guys turned up, the old man told them that having seen last night's shooting between their colleagues and the municipal police officers, he'd slept with one eye open. Especially with the rioting over at The 800. It's not very far from the rue Jean-Pierre-Stirbois to The 800, I don't know if you can picture it.'

'No, I can't.'

'Well it turns out that the bearded chap was a member of the second team in the bar de l'Amitié. Name of Malik Benghabrit.'

'Yes, I've heard of him. Good news, then?'

'Absolutely, Commissioner. There's just one left now.'

'Or maybe two.'

'One or two. You seem pensive, Commissioner?'

'A Mat 49 that's more than seventy years old, up against Benghrabit's Kalashnikov. Did pretty well for himself, that old man.'

'He did, didn't he?'

'Where is he now?'

'At the police station.'

'Would probably be a good idea to keep this quiet. I don't want our fascist friends making him into some kind of hero. And don't go prosecuting him for possession of an unlicensed weapon either, right? Best to keep that up your sleeve for now, until things calm down a bit.'

'My daughter's in her final year at the lycée Sainte-Geneviève.'

'What about it?'

'I'm worried.'

'I can understand that, but we've got the ESSP in place in every school in the city.'

'Yes, well you know what they say about the "ESSP"...'

'Yes I know, but don't worry, it'll all be over soon.'

14

Flavien Dubourg is ashamed of himself. He just couldn't help himself. Alizé Lavaux's arse. Really, what on earth was he thinking? If Alizé Lavaux had reacted, it would have really kicked off. His male students would have protested their innocence, and since they protest their innocence in exactly the same way whether they are innocent or not, nobody believes them anymore. There would have been pandemonium, especially with all the tension in the air, what with the heat and last night's events.

The Lower Sixth Sales class have finally taken their seats. Somebody has opened the windows, because it's like a hothouse in there. Of course, that means they get all the noise from the building site. Pneumatic drills, bulldozers, trucks lurching this way and that. They have to shout just to be heard.

As Flavien Dubourg feared, only three students have their questionnaires, and just four have brought their copy of the book. Stacy Billon has both. But what's she doing in that hippy dress that's as ugly as the one Flavien Dubourg's maternal grandmother is wearing in the family snapshots? Rather than the sleeveless top and mini-skirt Stacy Billon goes for as soon as the temperature gets above 10°C? It must be at least 25°C today, and Flavien Dubourg is really hacked off by the girl's eccentric fashion sense.

As for Alizé Lavaux, she's now removed her jacket. There are beads of perspiration on her upper lip, and the beginnings of sweat marks under the arms of her blue t-shirt. Flavien Dubourg likes that. He would like just about anything where Alizé Lavaux or Stacy Billon are concerned. Even if they didn't wash for a fortnight, and then offered themselves to him in a pigsty, he'd still like it. Flavien Dubourg suspects he might like it even more.

'So who would like to ask Alizé Lavaux the first question then? Karim?'

Karim doesn't have his copy of *Sun for Everyone!* with him. He borrows the questionnaire of the girl sitting next to him. Karim recites the question, written in somebody else's hand. What with the noise outside, nobody can hear what he says.

'Could you repeat that, Karim?' asks Flavien Dubourg.

Karim, dressed in a tracksuit of the football team from this port city in the West, sighs impatiently.

Alizé Lavaux tries to encourage him: 'It's always difficult when you're the first one, but go ahead, Karim...'

Alizé Lavaux addresses him by his first name. Alizé Lavaux is entitled to do this. There's her charisma as a writer, despite the hand on her bum a few minutes ago, not to mention the fact that she's from outside Charles-Tillon. Just as Karim reads out his question for a second time, a lorry full of gravel passes inches away from prefab hut no. 47. Dust comes in through the windows. The students cough exaggeratedly, although not entirely without reason. Flavien Dubourg is vaguely reminded of a scene from a film he once saw, he can't quite remember which one. Tati, Chaplin, an Italian comedy?

Karim tosses the sheet of questions petulantly onto the floor. The student who lent it him, Zakia, a small chubby girl who's dressed practically in full Islamic garb – all she'll have left to do to complete the outfit once she's back outside Charles-Tillon is put on a veil – complains as she bends down to pick it up: 'Fffucksake, Karim, be careful will you? I didn't lend you that questionnaire so you could throw it on the floor!'

Karim gets ready to hurl an insult. He opens his mouth, and Flavien Dubourg can practically hear the words that Karim will utter and which will trigger a real palaver, followed by an endless debate about respect for others.

Yes, Karim does indeed open his mouth to say 'Up yours, bitch!' but strangely enough, what comes out of his mouth is not an insult but an alarm.

An alarm which bursts the eardrums of everybody in prefab hut no. 47.

Flavien Dubourg is reminded of another film scene now, one he has no trouble identifying: it's the bit in *Body Snatchers* where Donald Sutherland realises his body has been taken over by aliens.

The alarm has a very distinctive ring: a note at maximum volume which rises and then falls, repeated three times, with five seconds between each note.

After the alarm, silence.

A real silence for once.

The temporary workers from Romania who were busy rebuilding the school have disappeared, as have their colleagues, the illegal immigrants from Mali. No more pneumatic drills, no more bulldozers, no more lorries.

'What the hell's going on now?' Alizé Lavaux blurts out.

Alizé Lavaux is getting a little tired of all of this. She could kill for another fag.

'It's like last week's exercise, isn't it?' asks Omar. 'What a fuckin' pain. I mean do they really think there'd be terrorists at Tillon?! *Wallah*, they're such pricks...'

'What about last night's riots, dickhead?' says Quoc Han.

Omar replies with a withering suck of the teeth, 'You always have to blame the Muslims don't you, you bloody spring roll. I bet you've just farted and they think there's a leak at the nuclear power station down the road.'

That makes everyone laugh.

'Don't you think things are getting a little out of hand?' asks Alizé Lavaux.

Flavien Dubourg feels deep despair, but tries to get a hold of himself. If he plays his cards right, once this is all over Alizé Lavaux might not think he's such a wimp after all. Alizé Lavaux might even want to talk about it with him, might see him as a kind of therapist. That would create a rapport between them, and thanks to that rapport he might finally get the chance to stick his dick up her ginger pussy, by God – by hook or by crook, it's all the same to him.

Flavien Dubourg addresses the entire room, in his most serious voice: 'We did indeed do the exercise last week, but since I haven't been told anything, there's every chance that this time it's for real! Let me remind you of the ESSP procedure. Omar, you close the windows – yes, I know it's hot in here, but never mind. And pull the curtains as well, or what's left of them. Everybody switch off your phones. Quoc Han, Karim, Frank – get that cupboard and put it behind the door. Stacy, get the first aid kit from the other cupboard, over there. Check which members of the class are here today. And note the names of everybody present on the pro forma. And don't forget Alizé Lavaux.'

'I need a wee!' This very dignified announcement is made by Kahina, who is currently on an internship at the reception desk of the Hermès boutique in the city centre, and who is not allowed to speak like that to her well-heeled customers who come from the Sainte-Marguerite area of town, or who live on the avenue Général-Leclerc.

Alizé Lavaux also needs a wee, but is too shy to say so. The situation seems totally surreal to her. So much so that she doesn't even recognise her own name on the copy of *Sun for Everyone!* right there in front of her.

All of a sudden, Flavien Dubourg is no longer afraid.

Strange as it may seem, Flavien Dubourg is actually quite a serious teacher. He continues to give instructions. Flavien Dubourg becomes increasingly convinced that yes, the situation is indeed a golden opportunity to cosy up to Alizé Lavaux.

'Everybody sit on the floor, now! And no talking.'

Flavien Dubourg finds himself sitting next to – right next to – Alizé Lavaux. She smells nice, a mixture of perspiration, perfume and tobacco. Flavien Dubourg looks closely at her freckles, and the grainy surface of her skin. He feels like licking her face.

Her face and the rest of her too.

Time goes by. This is taking longer than last week's exercise. After half an hour, the students begin to get restless. They're a bit scared but they're restless.

'Frank, I said phones off!'

'But it's on flight mode, sir!'

'I said phones off! Put it back in your bag.'

'Flight mode, my arse,' says Omar. 'Fright mode more like, you ugly bastard.'

Laughter breaks out among the students. All of them except for Kahina, who is desperate for a pee, and is squirming more and more frantically.

She pleads, 'I can't hold on any longer, M. Dubourg, I really can't. I need the toilet.'

'I'm sorry, Kahina...'

'But, sir...'

'Why don't you just go and do it over there in the corner?' Omar suggests helpfully.

'So you can get a good look at my arse...'

'I wouldn't be the first...'

More laughter breaks out, louder this time. Especially among the boys, of course.

Outside, the silence is deafening. It's nearly 11 o'clock.

15

It's also at 11 o'clock that Abdenour Van der Valk says to himself, 'Might as well go out with a bang.'

Abdenour Van der Valk, 23 years old, radicalised during his first stretch in prison for stealing a scooter, is the son of a Belgian labourer he never knew – or practically never – and a Tunisian woman who works in the children's department of the Nouvelles Galeries department store on the boulevard de l'Yser. Abdenour Van der Valk was a member of the second team sent by the Combatant on account of Abdul Slimane's hasty exit from the Youth Club premises at the very moment that they were discussing today's attack.

Sent to provide cover for the first team who were meant to silence Abdul Slimane.

Given the right mess that little episode's sparked, Abdenour Van der Valk is sorry they couldn't think of a more discreet way of dealing with Slimane. The situation was critical, but even so – where did the Combatant think he was, the bloody Caliphate?

There were three of them in the second team. Once they'd finished wreaking mayhem in the Bar de l'Amitié, they made a full report to the Combatant, by telephone. The Combatant told them to ditch the metallic brown BMW and then split up, making sure not to go back to The 800, because the place was bound to be crawling with cops. The Combatant had given them the address of a place in the Paris area that they could go to, for afterwards. After what exactly – well, that was anybody's guess. And anyway, it was too risky to leave now; they were bound to be spotted. So they had to sit tight and wait – but wait where, and how?

Malik Benghabrit had suggested Abdenour Van der Valk find himself a house occupied by old people to hide in – somewhere in the rue Pouget for example. Old people were deaf as doorposts, and the cops would never think of searching the rue Pouget. And of course the street was only a short walk away. Abdenour Van der Valk couldn't quite put his finger on it, but something told him that wasn't a very good idea.

Hacène Ali, the third member of the team, said he was going to stay with a girlfriend that nobody had heard of – not even the Combatant – a single French girl who had a loft, and who was a real stunner, so he reckoned. The two others thought Hacène Ali was making it all up. He was probably going to spend his time bumming around the place and hiding in bins, the daft Arab sod. Did he really think he could just turn up at some French girl's place with that stupid face of his and a Kalashnikov, and she'd drop her knickers, no questions asked?

The three men had gone their separate ways. Abdenour Van der Valk didn't know about Hacène Ali, but he'd been driven crazy that night, with all those sirens blaring and the patrol cars everywhere, their flashing lights painting the sky red above The 800, at the top of the Saint-François hill. Petrifying, it was. Abdenour Van der Valk had walked down towards the centre of town. Abdenour Van der Valk had managed to avoid the CCTV cameras at the road junctions and in front of the banks. Abdenour Van der Valk knew he was on the government's list of suspected terrorists, and all that bollocks.

Abdenour Van der Valk had eventually hidden in a large wheelie bin belonging to some posh villa, one of the yellow bins that are only emptied on Fridays. Abdenour Van der Valk had fallen asleep with his arms wrapped around his Kalashnikov. Inside that bin he had felt safe, as if he were inside a womb.

And now the sun is high in the sky and the city is under siege. Abdenour Van der Valk says his prayers near the wheelie bin, in the back yard of the house where nobody can see him.

Abdenour Van der Valk stinks of old cardboard boxes. He comes across pages from an old newspaper – not the local rag, something the chattering classes might read. Next to an ad for a concert by a rock group he's never heard of, he reads: *We could join forces, pool our bodily organs and fluids. You three, for example, might decide to be the sperm providers, and as such you would collect, and mix your sperm. We women might then decide that one of us should be inseminated by that sperm, and then once the child is born, pass it on to someone from outside the group. That's just how politics works.*

Abdenour Van der Valk thinks that's even filthier than porn. Unless of course it's meant to be funny. Either way, you'd have to look long and hard to find anything more *haram* than those very satanic verses. The Imam's right: the West really has gone to hell in a handcart.

Abdenour Van der Valk, had he not been distracted by this scrap of newsprint, might perhaps have noticed that he was only two streets away from the Nouvelles Galeries on the boulevard de l'Yser where his mother worked, although it was her day off today. Had he realised, might he have stopped running? Might he have decided to go and pump the last of his ammunition into the department store's customers, or would he have opted instead to give himself up?

We'd have to ask the omniscient narrator, although for the moment he seems to have gone AWOL.

So we'll just have to keep our eyes on Abdenour Van der Valk as he runs, carrying his Kalashnikov, past people screaming with fear and towards the department store, and listen as he utters quite redundant oaths about the one true God, while attempting to unclip the jammed magazine of his rifle before clipping it back in again.

We will follow him as he risks life and limb crossing the busy boulevard de l'Yser and then stops in front of the Art Nouveau façade of the Nouvelles Galeries (designed by architect Georges Chedanne in 1909, it is a rare example of what the port city in the West used to look like before the Allies bombed it), and we will watch as Abdenour Van der Valk, still grappling with his Kalashnikov's jammed magazine, is torn to shreds by bullets fired from the Fama assault rifles of two *Chasseurs Alpins* from the 27th Mountain Infantry Brigade, on patrol in the city as part of Operation Sentinel.

Abdenour Van der Valk's last thought, as 5.56 calibre bullets fired in bursts of three rounds at a time and travelling at 900 metres per second inflict irreparable damage to his vital organs and he collapses in front of Georges Chedanne's façade, is whether Hacène Ali really did spend last night with a French girl, and if her breasts were as beautiful as those belonging to the store's caryatide, who gazes down at him now with a strange kind of smile, and seems to be taking the mickey, quite honestly.

16

The reason why everything goes pear-shaped in prefab hut no. 47 at 11.15 has probably little to do with distant geopolitical conflicts, and everything to do with Kahina's need for a wee.

Or to be more precise, with Zakia, the girl sitting next to Kahina, who yells, 'Oh that's disgusting, Kahina! You've no consideration for other people! You've gone and wet yourself!'

'I said no talking!' Flavien Dubourg yells, just as loud.

'Easy for you to say – you're not the one sitting next to her!'

Kahina starts to cry, and her tears, on top of Zakia's selfishness, tip Flavien Dubourg literally over the edge. So much so that he forgets Alizé Lavaux's presence. He stands up and slaps Zakia across the face.

'Shut up, you stupid bitch!'

'Oh, sir, you can't do that, sir!' Those not very numerous, but nevertheless quite pugnacious, students from Flavien Dubourg's Lower Sixth Sales class present in the room exclaim as one.

Everybody's on their feet now, apart from Alizé Lavaux, who remains sitting on the floor, puts her head between her knees and locks her hands together at the nape of her neck, exhausted, and quite terrified.

Flavien Dubourg gets knocked about.

He even gets punched, a little, then quite a bit, and then

a hell of a lot. He's accused of racism, of Islamophobia, of practising sodomy with all manner of living creatures, that kind of thing. They say he struck Zakia because she is a sister who respects herself. Not like that slag Stacy or Kahina with those piss-stinking jogging pants.

'What did you say, Omar?' Quoc Han suddenly yells. 'Did you call Stacy a slag? Yer fucking coon! Yer two-faced twat!'

'I can fight my own battles,' says Stacy Billon.

'We'll just have to see about that, won't we? I'm gonna give yer one. And don't you dare move a muscle, Quoc Han! I'm gonna show you what a real man is, you fucking two-bit Jackie Chan!'

The epicentre of the violence is no longer Flavien Dubourg, who has blood dripping from his nose onto his torn linen jacket and whose right eye is swelling bigger by the minute.

Omar walks towards Stacy Billon, who is still standing there calmly with her back against one of the prefab's walls.

'It'll help pass the time, won't it, lads? We're gonna get our end away while we wait to get blown to bits by them blokes in beards. Carpe diem!' exclaims Omar Diop, who has suddenly become a disciple of Epicurus.

Alizé Lavaux is standing up now and heading towards the door. Alizé Lavaux is moving like a clockwork rabbit.

'I'm going to call for help...'

Flavien Dubourg is gobsmacked. He spits out a tooth. He's taken a bit of a pasting, and may well have pissed himself, like Kahina. Out of fear. Flavien Dubourg belongs to a generation that were no longer required to do National Service, and to a social class which doesn't frequent night clubs. Despite his radical tendencies, Flavien Dubourg has always found the behaviour of those marching at the front of political demonstrations to be completely irresponsible. Flavien Dubourg is twenty-seven years old, and although he is not necessarily a coward, he has never actually experienced physical violence. It is what it is. So he is a bit on automatic pilot now, as he stands there stunned, humiliated and feeling a little sick.

Seeing Alizé Lavaux about to go outside, the only thing Flavien Dubourg can find to say is something extremely bureaucratic: 'The ESSP is quite specific, Alizé; under no circumstances are we to leave the room until we hear the all-clear.'

'I couldn't give a toss. I need a pee and I need a smoke, and I have no desire to stand here and watch a gang rape. So you can stick your ESSP up your arse.'

Omar sends a table flying and rushes at Alizé Lavaux. Omar must be twice as big as her, and three times as heavy. He grabs hold of the author's short ginger hair, and her Converse sneakers slide along the lino floor as he drags her to the back of the prefab.

Alizé Lavaux is too stunned to yell.

'Did you hear what the teacher said, bitch?'

We can safely assume that Omar's words and deeds are not exactly motivated by a sudden respect for authority. Indeed, he then goes on to say, 'We're going to sit here nice and quiet and wait for the all-clear, right? And we're going to fuck Stacy – and we'll fuck you too if you give us any more trouble. And then, once the alert's over, we'll all of us keep our traps well and truly shut – that includes you, Mr Teacher. Because what goes on inside hut 47 stays inside hut 47. And that goes for you too, you Parisian bitch. You can run, but you can't hide. I've got loads of cousins in Paris, me! Frank, Karim, hold her down for me while I shag Stacy nice and slow. What do you reckon then, Stacy?'

Stacy Billon, standing there in her Jefferson Airplane dress, looks about as impassive as it's possible to be. So impassive in fact, that Omar suddenly feels terrified. Stacy Billon stares at him, but it's as if she can't actually see him. She stares at him, in fact, as if he were already dead. Omar's appetite for sexual intercourse suddenly vanishes. He briefly considers forcing Stacy to get down on her knees and take him in her mouth in an effort to revive his dormant anaconda, but realises it wouldn't make any difference.

Omar turns towards Alizé Lavaux being held firmly down on a table by Frank and Karim. Omar's going to shag her instead. It's the only way he'll be able to get rid of the very unpleasant feeling that Stacy Billon has given him. Like some kind of fucking spell, some shamanistic evil eye.

Alizé Lavaux is squirming now too.

'Cut the crap, Omar,' says Quoc Han. 'Unless you want some of this.'

Quoc is holding a large Stanley knife in his hand. The kind used for slicing through wallpaper, or carpet.

Flavien Dubourg, who's still a bit lost, can find nothing better to say than, 'Quoc Han, Stanley knives are only allowed in the workshops, and anyway you're doing Sales! I'm afraid I'm going to have to report this.'

Flavien Dubourg has lost it completely.

Kahina laughs nervously.

So does Omar.

The nervous laughter starts to spread, and quite soon everybody's laughing.

Everyone, that is, except for Stacy Billon, her gaze as ironic and impenetrable as ever, and Alizé Lavaux, who is still trying to free herself from the firm hold Frank and Karim have on her – and Flavien Dubourg, who looks for all the world as though he doesn't understand anything, and who in fact doesn't understand anything.

Truth be told, if Flavien Dubourg were a boxer in a ring, his trainer, seeing him suffering from severe concussion, would have thrown in the towel by now.

It's at that point that they hear the first bursts of gunfire, dangerously close.

Bullets shatter the windows of prefab hut no. 47, causing tiny fragments of glass and plastic to fly through the room and injure more or less everybody to a certain degree. Most of all Flavien Dubourg, who's the only one who didn't fling himself onto the floor.

Nobody's laughing anymore.

17

The reason why Hacène Ali finds himself in the warehouse of a furniture store has to do, first of all, with the fact that – as Abdenour Van der Valk and Malik Benghabrit suspected – there never was a woman crazy enough about him to wait for him in her loft on the other side of town.

No. Hacène Ali has simply remembered that three years ago he landed a temporary job in this store, shifting furniture. A non-renewable temporary job, but he still has the code for the loading bay door, and was relieved to see that the code hadn't changed.

Hacène Ali kept out of sight of the store's security staff and slipped into the warehouse, where he meditated for a few hours, surrounded by suede sofas under their plastic sheeting, available for three easy payments and destined to furnish the three-piece dreams of the middle classes of this port city in the West.

His plan is to steal a car somewhere in this retail park as soon as the sun is up and shoot on down to Paris, to the address the Combatant gave him. Or he might, since it's just round the corner, head over to Charles-Tillon and kill a few people. That wouldn't be quite as spectacular as the attack that he was due to take part in alongside the Little Rebel, but she's probably had a change of heart anyway, given the way things have turned out.

Hacène Ali hasn't slept a wink all night. Hacène Ali is full of the Captagon that he brought back from one of his trips to the Syrian-Turkish border. He pops his last pill. He hasn't slept in about forty hours, but he's OK. He's fine. Hacène Ali feels invincible, and so goes for the Charles-Tillon option.

At least Hacène Ali will die a martyr's death.

He knows that the lycée is pretty near the retail park, about two kilometres away. It'll be no trouble for Hacène Ali to make his way through the warehouses, the lorry parks, the petrol stations and the scrawny vegetation, avoiding the security cameras. He knows the area well; he broke into a few places and stole one or two cars round here before finding his true vocation thanks to Holy Jihad.

Before the morning shift arrives to open up the store, Hacène Ali slips out of the warehouse. He has folded away the barrel of his Kalashnikov, and stowed the weapon in his rucksack. He's taken off his woolly hat, and his white sleeveless jacket. He's dressed in jeans and t-shirt now. Apart from the beard, he might almost be mistaken for something else. Almost, but not quite.

Hacène Ali makes good progress. He does however find it necessary, near a motel, to stab a security guard and his dog who are barring his way towards the first huts of the building site at Charles-Tillon, which is not very far now. The struggle is brief: the security guard is a young lad, a frighteningly scrawny, spotty youth. His hand goes towards the teargas canister at his belt when he spots Hacène Ali whip out his switchblade, but he's much too slow, for he's from a temping agency and has not been trained for this kind of thing. As for the dog, it's wearing a muzzle so as not to upset the motel's customers. Before he dies, the guard just manages to unfasten the dog's muzzle. The damn thing gives Hacène Ali a nasty bite on the arm, but he barely notices, thanks to the Captagon he's taken. Hacène Ali just sees the blood falling in big drops onto the car park tarmac, before dealing with the dog with the same aplomb as that with which he dispatched the guard.

It's the dog's whining which attracts the attention of the motel's only customers, a couple of sales reps who are having an illicit affair and were just enjoying a last quick shag before leaving their room and making up tall stories to explain to their respective spouses why they haven't phoned home.

The adulterous couple, a thirty-five-year-old woman from Orléans who works in insurance and a forty-three-year-old man from Brive who works for a pharmaceutical company, met in the retail park's steakhouse. After their third cocktail, they decided to go to bed: they'd had more than enough of work for one day.

During the lovemaking which both of them found more or less satisfying, the television in the room had been left on, tuned to a twenty-four-hour news channel with the sound off. In the morning, while he was taking her from behind, they had seen that tensions were high in the port city in the West where they were staying.

That hadn't put an end to their fun, although at the time she suggested that it wouldn't be worth them staying in the port city for another day, since nobody would feel like buying insurance or vitamin supplements in a place rife with rioting and terrorist shootings.

'They really piss me off though,' the man said while trying not to come, as she was nowhere near reaching orgasm yet.

18

As the dog gives a last heart-rending whine, the adulterous couple – who since their day is fucked haven't bothered to get dressed yet even though it's already 9.20 – look out of their window. A silhouetted figure disappears behind the hedge of their motel car park, and there's a dog and a security guard lying dead in the car park. They're both covered in blood.

It's the woman who calls the cops. She looks at the man in the room with her. They're both thinking the same thing: police interviews, etc. Their chances of remaining anonymous are about as non-existent as the vital signs of the guard and his dog. But they can't just pretend it didn't happen. They're responsible citizens, even if it's a bloody shame that they're going to have to sacrifice their respective marriages in the name of the war against terrorism. To be honest, at this precise moment, they reckon that they're just two more collateral victims of that particular war.

As for the cops, after they get the woman's call, they put two and two together pretty fast. In the Crisis Room, the local Director for Public Safety, the senior police officer – who's still sweating just as profusely – and the man from the French Directorate for Internal Security congratulate themselves that the ESSP is in place at Charles-Tillon. Even if it wasn't, they would still have more than enough time to send in a Special Firearms unit to intercept Hacène Ali once he gets to the lycée.

Based on a computer projection of his path from the motel at the retail park, Hacène Ali should arrive at Charles-Tillon via the southern edge of the building site, where the first occupied temporary building which the jihadist will target is prefab hut no. 47. This can be seen on the plan of the lycée scanned by the Deputy Head now barricaded in his office and emailed straight to the iPads of the officials in the Crisis Room, and to the Head of the Special Firearms unit who will shortly arrive on the scene. All it needs is one marksman in an elevated position, in a crane for example, and Bob's your uncle.

Except that, what with his knowledge of the area and the effects of the Captagon, Hacène Ali arrives sooner than anticipated – at precisely the same time as the Special Firearms unit.

Nothing can stop a bloodbath now.

A police helicopter relays the images. It's all over after just a few seconds, although the terrorist manages to hit prefab hut no. 47 before he's shot dead and falls into a hole where he ends up impaled on iron rods sticking out of some reinforced concrete.

Still, there's relief. The second team have been eliminated. They've won.

Everybody in the Crisis Room – apart from the local Director for Public Safety, who's not very tactile – gives each other high-fives, a bit like NASA technicians when they launch a rocket into space, you know the kind of thing.

19

Stacy Billon is relieved. It'll all be over soon.

The smell in prefab hut no. 47 was beginning to get really bad. Urine, sweat, dust. And Stacy Billon's boiling under that thing she's wearing. It's heavy too, it hurts her hips like hell, and she's got a sharp pain in her back.

Whatever lingering doubts Stacy Billon may have had before, they have all evaporated by now. What she has seen since nine o'clock that morning is pathetic. The sex-mad teacher knocked about and humiliated, with appalling cuts to his face caused by flying shards of glass. That ginger-haired woman with her novel, *Sun for Everyone!* It's not bad, but she really is one stuck-up cow, that Alizé Lavaux! Those retards Karim and Frank daren't even look at her. The same goes for Omar and Quoc Han, who gets up now as instructed by the voice coming through the megaphone outside. He's still holding the Stanley knife in his hand.

Omar, that pathetic, shifty fat kid, tries to save face: 'The cops are going to come in here now. Like I said, what happens in hut no. 47 stays in hut no. 47.' Omar could have got himself killed, but that's not what's bothering him. What's bothering him is that he's more or less responsible for what's gone on in there. Stacy Billon is sure he would have raped her, just to piss off Quoc Han, and he would have raped Alizé Lavaux too.

Omar, my poor Omar, you just had to ask, at least where I'm

concerned. I would have said yes. You boys look so peaceful afterwards. Like babies after they've had their milk. You look almost sweet, you who spend the rest of your time acting real hard, playing the tough guy. Stacy Billon remembers that story her biology teacher told the class one day about the alpha male. Never a truer word spoken.

A shame really, because he could have been all right, Flavien Dubourg. Stacy Billon almost regained her faith in humanity, seeing the effort he used to go to whenever he wanted to talk to them about his favourite literary texts. There was something beautiful about it, noble even, and she thinks she could even have talked to him about Rimbaud. The little faggot poet from the Ardennes has been in her system since she was thirteen. But then what difference would it have made, talking?

It's the same for that other prick, with his Qur'an and his verses that Stacy Billon pretended to chant. Could Rimbaud have changed him? Stacy Billon doesn't think so. And yet – *He amused himself by cutting the throats of rare beasts. He set palaces on fire. He threw himself at people and cut them to pieces* – he might have understood that bit of Rimbaud.

No, not really. He was too bloody stupid. And to think he believed that he was the one manipulating her... He never suspected, not even for a second, that it was the other way around, that Stacy Billon has been observing everything going on in The 800 from the day she was born, and knew exactly who he was. Whereas the cops with all their informants were never able to spot him.

It was Stacy Billon who had galvanised him – cautiously, gradually, to make him believe that the submissive Little Rebel was enthralled with the Combatant. But what attracted Stacy Billon to him was the knowledge that one way or another he would enable her to go out with a bang, to tell them in the most spectacular way possible 'I hate you all!'

She is perfectly calm and serene when she thinks about death. When the investigators break into her room after knocking her mother out of the way, her mother doped up on her anti-depressants and her super-strength lager, they'll find her diary. Stacy Billon's been keeping a diary since she was four years old. Onto those pages she pours out her frustration, her anger, her life. She doesn't spend hours on social media, but prefers A5 sheets of paper with their neat little squares, and their margin delineated by a single vertical red line, the black ink for those fountain pens of hers she buys in the newsagent's at the station, because that's the only place she can find them.

The cops in their dark uniforms, their helmets and their masks burst in, their movements calm, precise.

They bark orders: head down, run towards the assembly station, in front of the new buildings. Stacy Billon sees other groups of students, escorted by other teams of police. There are ambulances too, helicopters, cars and vans from the television news channels.

Stacy Billon is standing right in the middle of it all; there are so many people she can hardly move, and the heat is stifling. The clocks will soon be striking midday in this port city in the West.

Stacy catches Alizé Lavaux's eye, then a cop's.

It looks like they know, each in their own way. She has the impression Alizé Lavaux is asking her why. More precisely, she is asking why, but no sound comes out of her mouth. Alizé Lavaux merely has the pathetic look on her face of someone who understands too late, but who doesn't hold it against her. Stacy Billon would have liked to be able to give her the chance to smoke one last cigarette, but the situation's going to escalate very quickly from here on in.

Stacy Billon has the detonator switch in her hand.

She knows exactly what to do. The Combatant was a bad lover with all his hang-ups, but an excellent bomb maker, and a first-rate teacher when it came to showing her how to kill with TATP. The latest, state-of-the-art explosive and the bomb ingredient of choice for jihadists, she has ten little sticks of this Triacetone Triperoxide that looks like putty strapped around her waist, and the only thing she was a bit frightened of was the heat, since that's something to which TATP is very sensitive. It really wouldn't have been ideal if things had dragged on too long in that prefab hut.

The cop who's understood yells something, and gesticulates in an effort to get everybody to move out of the way. Empty space begins to appear slowly, too slowly, around Stacy Billon.

A bullet hits her square in the forehead, but too late to prevent her from flicking the detonator switch.

20

Among the thirty-one dead were all those present in prefab hut no. 47, with the exception of Flavien Dubourg, who was on his way to hospital in an ambulance at the time.

Among the one hundred and forty-three wounded were a number of students, teachers, police officers, medics and journalists from the television news channels, including one very well-known reporter.

The first new buildings at Charles-Tillon, which had only just been completed, now resembled the kind of thing one might see at a school in Baghdad or Afghanistan, or even Syria – which had the effect of bringing those distant geopolitical conflicts very close to home indeed.

Despite feelings running particularly high, anti-Muslim reaction was on the whole quite guarded during the days following the attack. It was only when investigators from the French Directorate for Internal Security discovered the two thousand pages of notes written by Stacy-the-Suicide-Bomber while cloistered in her bedroom in a tower block in The 800 that the shit really hit the fan.

They contained nothing of any use to investigators on terrorist networks themselves. What they did reveal, on the other hand, was the way in which Stacy Billon had used the Islamists living in The 800 to help her carry out her attack on the school.

As this didn't quite fit any neo-reactionary theory, the usual harbingers of the Decline of the West, of the Clash of Civilisations, and of the Great Replacement cried foul. Billon's 'notes', they screamed, were no more authentic than *The Protocols of the Learned Elders of Zion*. And later on, when the authenticity of *The Little Rebel's Manuscripts* – as these notes gradually came to be called – was proven beyond doubt, those same people accused the teachers and the educators, those who had manned the barricades in May '68 and the supporters of assisted parenthood for gay couples, of having spent more than fifty years systematically destroying the very soul of France, indoctrinating the country's youth with a terrifying nihilism which was no less a threat than Islamism, and indeed served precisely the same ends.

The Little Rebel's Manuscripts were eventually published by a press known for publishing work by supporters of the New Age communities who live on the Plateau de Millevaches in Central France.

And it was in the 2080s, when Stacy Billon's *oeuvre* finally achieved a literary status close to that of le Comte de Lautréamont's *The Dirges of Maldoror*, or Rimbaud's *A Season in Hell*, that the first PhD on her work was written, entitled *Nihilism, Sexuality and Metaphor in the Work of Stacy Billon*, by a student named Simon Dubourg, the grandson of our Flavien Dubourg, who managed to land on his feet, as it were, shortly after the tragic events.

Which just goes to show.

Note: The extract read by Abdenour Van de Valk when he steps out of the wheelie bin is from 'Boiling Fluids', an interview with Beatriz Preciado, published in the journal *Vacarmes*, dated 23 April 2013.